THE CAVES

SPIDER

D0812772

BENJAMIN HULME-CROSS

Illustrated by
Nelson Evergreen

Thurrock Council

3013020913194 4

First published 2014 by A & C Black,
an imprint of Bloomsbury Publishing Plc
50 Bedford Square
London WC1B 3DP
Bloomsbury is a registered trademark of Bloomsbury Publishing Plc

www.bloomsbury.com

Copyright © 2014 A & C Black
Text copyright © 2014 Benjamin Hulme-Cross
Illustrations copyright © 2014 Nelson Evergreen

The right of Benjamin Hulme-Cross and Nelson Evergreen to be identified as
the author and illustrator of this work has been asserted by them
in accordance with the Copyrights, Designs and Patents Act 1988.

ISBN 978-1-4729-0093-7

A CIP catalogue for this book is available from the British Library.

All rights reserved. No part of this publication may be
reproduced in any form or by any means – graphic, electronic
or mechanical, including photocopying, recording, taping or
information storage and retrieval systems – without the prior
permission in writing of the publishers.

Printed and bound in India by Replika Press Pvt Ltd

1 3 5 7 9 10 8 6 4 2

The Teens can choose prison for life … or they can go on a game show called The Caves.

If the Teens beat the robot monsters, they go free. If they lose, they die.

I am Zak. Sometimes I help the Teens. Sometimes I don't.

The Teens were called Tom and Nicky. They looked scared. They ran to the caves.

The Voice spoke.

"The game begins in 10 minutes."

"Don't be afraid," said Tom.

"But most people die here," Nicky said. "And we didn't do anything wrong."

"I know," said Tom.

I thought Tom and Nicky were telling the truth.
I wanted to help them.

I took a metal spike and a blanket out of my bag
and put them on the ground.

I went outside. There was a cage on the rocks.
The spider was inside the cage.

It had eight long metal legs, sharp metal fangs, and a gun in its head.

The cage door opened and the spider ran into the caves. I went after it.

I could not see the Teens.

The blanket landed on my head. I fell
to the ground.

Tom stood over me. He had the spike
in his hand.

"Don't hit me!" I said. "I won't hurt you!
The spider is coming."

I told them, "The spider can bite you. It can shoot
you with its gun. Blind it with the blanket. Break
it with the spike."

The spider ran in. Its head turned. Its gun pointed at Tom.

I threw the blanket at the spider.

I climbed up the rocks, out of the way.

The spider fired its gun at Nicky but it could not see. It missed.

Tom jumped forward. He held the spike like
a spear.

He hit the spider with the spike. But it did not
hurt the spider.

The spider twisted and turned. The blanket fell off its head. The Teens saw its metal fangs.

The spider bit Tom's leg. He screamed.

Nicky ran up. She held a big rock over her head. She threw it down at the spider.

The spider's head smashed. It stopped moving.

Tom pulled the spider's fang out of his leg.

He said to Nicky, "You saved me!"

Nicky hugged him.

We heard the Voice.

"Game Over!"

Read more of

THE CAVES

SERIES

DOGS

DRONE

LION

LIZARD

SNAKE

SPIDER